Hamlet
Prince of Denmark

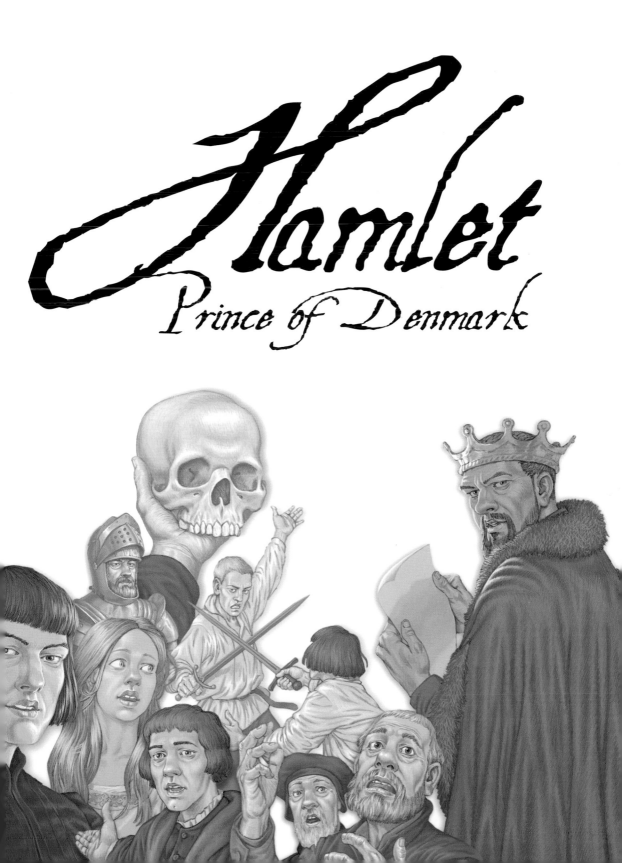

Artists: Penko Gelev
Sotir Gelev

First edition for North America (including Canada and Mexico),
Philippine Islands, and Puerto Rico published in 2009
by Barron's Educational Series, Inc.

All inquiries should be addressed to:
Barron's Educational Series, Inc.
250 Wireless Blvd.
Hauppauge, NY 11788
www.barronseduc.com

ISBN-13 (Hardcover): 978-0-7641-6145-2
ISBN-10 (Hardcover): 0-7641-6145-8
ISBN-13 (Paperback): 978-0-7641-4013-6
ISBN-10 (Paperback): 0-7641-4013-2

Library of Congress Control No.: 2008936596

Picture credits:
p. 40 TopFoto.co.uk
p. 42 John James
p. 47 © 2005 TopFoto/TopFoto.co.uk
Every effort has been made to trace copyright holders. The Salariya Book Company apologizes for any
omissions and would be pleased, in such cases, to add an acknowledgment in future editions.

Printed and bound in China
9 8 7 6 5 4 3 2 1

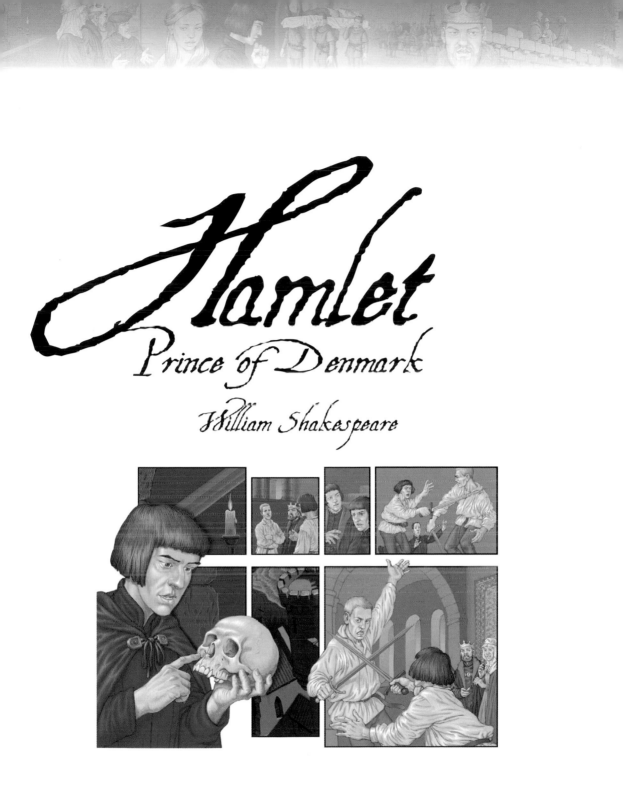

Hamlet
Prince of Denmark
William Shakespeare

Illustrated by

Penko Gelev

Retold by

Kathy McEvoy

Series created and designed by

David Salariya

The castle of Elsinore in Denmark, sometime in the twelfth century…

The old king, Hamlet, has recently died. He has been succeeded not by his son, Prince Hamlet, but by his brother, Claudius.

Claudius has married Gertrude, who is the old king's widow and Prince Hamlet's mother.

CHARACTERS

Hamlet,
Prince of Denmark

The Ghost of old Hamlet,
late King of Denmark,
Prince Hamlet's father

Claudius, new King of Denmark,
Hamlet's uncle and stepfather

Gertrude, Queen of Denmark,
Hamlet's mother

Horatio, Hamlet's friend
from the university

Polonius,
a courtier

Ophelia,
Polonius' daughter

Laertes,
Polonius' son

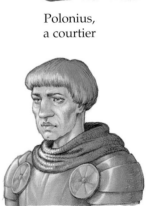

Fortinbras,
Prince of Norway

Rosencrantz and Guildenstern,
friends of Hamlet from childhood

A gravedigger

A WEIRD VISITOR

'Tis now struck twelve. Get thee to bed, Francisco.

For this relief, much thanks. 'Tis bitter cold, and I am sick at heart.

At midnight, the soldiers change guard on the battlements of the castle.

Has this thing appeared again tonight?

I have seen nothing.

Horatio has come to investigate two reported sightings of a ghost in recent nights.

Horatio says 'tis but our fantasy, and will not let belief take hold of him. Therefore I have entreated him along.[1]

Horatio does not believe in ghosts.

Look, where it comes again!

In the same figure,[2] like the king that's dead.

They begin to tell Horatio about the ghost when suddenly...

What art thou that usurp'st[3] this time of night? By heaven I charge thee, speak!

Horatio challenges the ghost, but it turns and disappears.

Is it not like the king?

As thou art to thyself.[4]

They all agree that the ghost looks very much like old Hamlet, who has just died.

...to recover of us... those foresaid lands so by his father lost.

Is it a warning that Prince Fortinbras of Norway plans to invade Denmark?

Stay, illusion! If thou hast any sound, or use of voice, speak to me.

The ghost reappears, and again Horatio tries to speak to it, but a cock crows. The ghost vanishes. It's dawn.

Let us impart what we have seen tonight unto young Hamlet. For, upon my life, this spirit, silent to us, will speak to him.

1. entreated him along: convinced him to come along.   2. In the same figure: In the same shape and form (as the old king).
3. usurp'st: invades or wrongfully takes over.   4. As thou art to thyself: As real as you are to yourself.

AN UNHAPPY PRINCE

> Though yet of Hamlet our dear brother's death the memory be green[1]...

Claudius is addressing the court and visitors who have come for the old king's funeral. Many still mourn him.

> Our sometime sister,[2] now our queen, have we, with mirth in funeral and with dirge in marriage,[3] taken to wife.

Claudius explains that, although he is grief-stricken, his marriage to Gertrude will keep the kingdom stable.

> Nor have we herein barr'd your better wisdoms,[4] which have freely gone with this affair along.

He thanks everyone for their good wishes and support.

> He hath not failed to pester us with message importing the surrender of those lands lost by his father.

> To suppress his further gait herein,[5] we here dispatch you, good Cornelius, and you, Voltemand.

He sends two ambassadors to Norway to negotiate with young Fortinbras, who threatens to invade.

> You told us of some matter. What is't, Laertes?

> My lord, your leave and favor[6] to return to France.

Laertes, the son of Polonius, wishes to return to his studies in France.

> Have you your father's leave? What says Polonius?

> He hath, my lord, wrung from me my slow leave by laborsome petition.[7]

Claudius asks Polonius if he approves of this...

> Laertes, time be thine, and thy best graces spend it at thy will.

...and agrees to let Laertes go.

---

1. green: fresh.   2. sometime sister: former sister-in-law.   3. with . . . marriage: with joy and sorrow at the same time.
4. barr'd your better wisdoms: ignored your good advice.   5. To suppress his further gait herein: to stop his progress.
6. leave and favor: permission.   7. laborsome petition: persistent requests.

But now, my nephew Hamlet, and my son—How is it that the clouds still hang on you?

Claudius questions Hamlet about his deep depression since his father's death.

A little more than kin, and less than kind.

"Son?" thinks Hamlet: we may be related by marriage, but we are not alike.

Good Hamlet, cast thy nighted color off.[1]

All that lives must die, passing through nature to eternity.

Gertrude tells her son that the time for grieving and wearing black is over, and he should welcome Claudius.

But I have that within which passes slow—these but the trappings and the suits of woe.[2]

Hamlet's grief is locked inside him, whatever color he wears.

To persevere in obstinate condolement[3] is a course of impious stubbornness.

Hamlet is accused of over-reacting—he should accept that death is a natural end.

Throw to earth this unprevailing woe.[4]

Let not thy mother lose her prayers[5]—stay with us. Go not to Wittenberg.

Claudius and Gertrude beg Hamlet not to return to his university in Wittenberg.

I shall in all my best obey you, madam.

Reluctantly, Hamlet agrees.

1. cast . . . off: remove your mourning clothes.   2. suits of woe: mourning clothes.   3. obstinate condolement: stubborn, continuous mourning.   4. Throw . . . woe: End this grief, no good will come of it.
5. lose her prayers: beg in vain.

A FRIEND IN NEED

O, that this too too solid flesh would melt, thaw and resolve itself into a dew. Or that the Everlasting had not fixed his canon 'gainst self-slaughter![1]

Hamlet is so unhappy he wants to die and disappear. Suicide would solve his problems—but it is a sin.

Frailty, thy name is woman!

How could his mother marry barely a month after his father's death?

Within a month... My father's brother, but no more like my father than I to Hercules.

My lord, I came to see your father's funeral.

I think it was to see my mother's wedding.

But just then Horatio and the soldiers burst in. Hamlet is glad to see his friend. He's sarcastic about the hasty marriage.

Indeed, my lord, it followed hard upon.

The funeral baked meats did coldly furnish forth the marriage tables.[2]

My lord, I think I saw him yesternight.[3]

Saw? Who?

My lord, the king, your father.

And then Horatio tells Hamlet about the ghost he has seen.

Thrice he walked by their oppressed and fear-surprised eyes!

I will watch tonight, perchance 'twill walk again.

Hamlet will keep watch himself tonight. Perhaps the ghost wants to warn him of something.

My father's spirit in arms![4] All is not well... Foul deeds will rise, though all the earth o'erwhelm them to men's eyes.[5]

Hamlet suspects the ghost's appearance has something to do with his father's death.

1. fixed . . . self-slaughter: forbidden suicide. 2. The funeral . . . tables: The leftover food from the funeral was served cold at the wedding. 3. yesternight: last night. 4. in arms: wearing armor. 5. Foul . . . eyes: Evil deeds will be found out, however carefully they are hidden.

My necessaries are embarked,[1] farewell. Do not sleep, but let me hear from you.

Laertes prepares to leave for France. He is very close to his sister Ophelia and is sorry to leave her.

For Hamlet and the trifling of his favor,[2] hold it a fashion and a toy in blood,[3] sweet, not lasting.

He warns her that Hamlet's feelings for her cannot be trusted.

His will is not his own... for on his choice depends the sanity and health of this whole state.

Then weigh what loss your honor may sustain[4] if, with too credent ear[5] you list[6] his songs, or lose your heart.

This above all: to thine own self be true.

Polonius now gives his son some fatherly advice: always be honest to yourself...

And it must follow, as the night the day, thou canst not then be false to any man.

...and others. Laertes sets off for France.

What is between you? Give me up the truth.

He hath, my lord, of late made many tenders[7] of his affection to me.

Polonius has overheard Laertes mention Hamlet. He questions Ophelia about the prince.

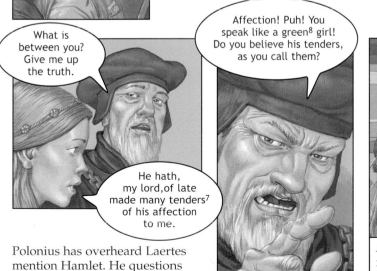

Affection! Puh! You speak like a green[8] girl! Do you believe his tenders, as you call them?

I would not, in plain terms, from this time forth, have you so slander any moment leisure,[9] as to give words or talk with the Lord Hamlet.

Angered, he forbids her to meet or talk with Hamlet. Meekly she obeys.

1. My necessaries are embarked: My belongings have been loaded on board ship.   2. the trifling of his favor: the unreliability of his affections.   3. a toy in blood: a whim of passion.   4. weigh what loss your honor may sustain: consider the honor you would lose.   5. with too credent ear: too trustingly.   6. list: listen to.   7. tenders: offers, expressions.   8. green: inexperienced, naïve.   9. slander any moment leisure: waste any of your time.

THE GHOST WALKS AGAIN

The clock strikes midnight.

> It then draws near the season[1] wherein the spirit held his wont to walk.[2]

Hamlet and his friends await the ghost on the battlements.

The sound of gunshots and a loud party is coming from the castle below.

> The king doth wake tonight and takes his rouse.[3]

> They clepe[4] us drunkards.

Hamlet is disgusted. His uncle's drunken and rowdy behavior is giving Denmark a bad reputation.

> Look, my lord, it comes!

Suddenly, the ghost appears!

> I'll call thee Hamlet, King, father, royal Dane.

> O answer me!

Hamlet speaks to his father's ghost.

> It beckons you to go away with it alone.

> Do not go with it.

> What if it tempt you toward the flood, my lord, or to the dreadful summit of the cliff?

> Unhand me, gentlemen! By heaven, I'll make a ghost of him that lets[5] me!

The others try to restrain him but Hamlet follows the ghost.

> Something is rotten in the state of Denmark. Let's follow him.

1. draws near the season: comes close to the time. 2. wherein the spirit held his wont to walk: when the spirit walks.
3. takes his rouse: is celebrating. 4. clepe: call. 5. lets: hinders.

I am thy father's spirit, doomed for a certain term to walk the night.

The serpent that did sting thy father's life now wears his crown.

My uncle!

Claudius poured poison into the king's ear as he slept.

Thus was I, sleeping, by a brother's hand, of life, of crown, of queen, at once dispatched.[1]

The king was killed by a "snake": his own brother!

Taint not thy mind, nor let thy soul contrive against thy mother aught.[2] Leave her to heaven.

Adieu, adieu, adieu. Remember me.

Never make known what you have seen tonight.

Thy commandment all alone shall live within the book and volume of my brain.[3]

At dawn the ghost vanishes. Hamlet's suspicions are correct.

The time is out of joint.[5] O cursed spite, that ever I was born to set it right!

There are more things in heaven and earth, Horatio, than are dreamt of in your philosophy.

I hereafter shall think to put an antic disposition on.[4]

Horatio can hardly believe what they've seen. Hamlet warns them that his behavior may become erratic.

With threats of an imminent invasion from Norway, can Hamlet avenge his father's murder?

1. dispatched: deprived.   2. aught: anything   3. within . . . brain: shall fill my mind.   4. think to put an antic disposition on: feel the need to act strangely.   5. The time is out of joint: The situation is bad.

Is Hamlet Mad?

1. with his doublet all unbraced: with his jacket undone.   2. He falls . . . draw it: He studies my face as if he were trying to draw it.   3. repel: refuse to take.   4. beshrew my jealousy: shame on my suspiciousness.

Claudius wants Hamlet's old friends to find out what's wrong with him.

Is Hamlet upset about something unknown to Claudius?

They are, after all, Hamlet's closest friends.

And their efforts will be rewarded...

As they leave, Polonius arrives with news.

The ambassadors have been successful. The king of Norway has made Prince Fortinbras a promise not to attack Denmark.

Fortinbras asks for safe passage through Denmark on his way to fight the Poles.

1. did . . . sending: made us send for you quickly.   2. to whom he more adheres: whom he trusts more.
3. our brother Norway: the king of Norway.   4. to give the assay of arms: to use weapons.

MAD OR LOVESICK?

He tells me... he hath found the head and source of all your son's distemper.[1]

Polonius thinks he can explain Hamlet's behavior.

"Doubt thou the stars are fire, doubt that the sun doth move...

He reads them a letter received by Ophelia.

Came this from Hamlet to her?

"Doubt truth to be a liar, but never doubt I love."

"Lord Hamlet is a prince out of thy star.[2] This must not be."

He had told Ophelia to give Hamlet up because she could never marry a Prince.

And he, repelled[3]... fell into a sadness, then... into the madness wherein now he raves.

He thinks Ophelia's rejection has driven Hamlet mad.

You know, sometimes he walks four hours together here in the lobby.

He suggests that they set a trap for Hamlet, to spy on him.

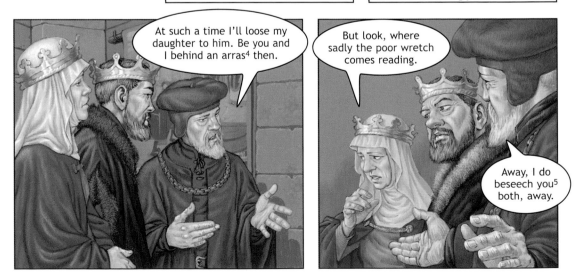

At such a time I'll loose my daughter to him. Be you and I behind an arras[4] then.

But look, where sadly the poor wretch comes reading.

Away, I do beseech you[5] both, away.

1. distemper: strange behavior.   2. out of thy star: not in your destiny.   3. repelled: rejected by Ophelia.
4. arras: tapestry wall hanging (made at Arras in northern France).   5. beseech you: beg you.

Do you know me, my lord?

Excellent well. You are a fishmonger.[1]

What do you read, my lord?

Words, words, words.

Yourself, sir, shall grow old as I am, if like a crab you could go backward.

Though this be madness, yet there is method in't.

Polonius soon sees for himself Hamlet's strange behavior.

Polonius suspects there's something behind this nonsense.

My honorable lord, I will most humbly take my leave of you.

Rosencrantz and Guildenstern have managed to find Hamlet.

Their sudden visit makes Hamlet suspicious.

You cannot, sir, take from me anything that I will more willingly part withal,[2] except my life.

How dost thou, Guildenstern? Ah, Rosencrantz! Good lads, how do ye both?

What make you[3] at Elsinore?

To visit you, my lord, no other occasion.

There is a kind of confession in your looks which your modesties[4] have not craft enough to color.[5]

He that plays the king shall be welcome...

You are welcome, but my uncle-father and aunt-mother are deceived.

I am mad but north-north-west. When the wind is southerly I know a hawk from a handsaw.[6]

To distract him, they announce the arrival of his favorite troupe of strolling actors.

Hamlet informs them that he knows what they're up to.

1. You are a fishmonger: Hamlet, pretending to be mad, claims not to recognize Polonius. 2. withal: with. 3. What make you?: What are you doing? 4. modesties: sense of shame.
5. have not craft enough to color: are not crafty enough to hide.
6. I know a hawk from a handsaw: I know what's what.

THE ACTORS

Polonius announces the actors. They can perform any style of acting one can name.

The best actors in the world, either for tragedy, comedy, history, pastoral...

Pray God, your voice, like a piece of uncurrent[1] gold, be not cracked within the ring.[2]

Hamlet teases the boy who plays the women's parts—soon his voice will break.

Come, give us a taste of your quality. Come, a passionate speech.

Hamlet is impatient for them to begin.

Look where he has not turned his color and has tears in's eyes.

The lead actor performs a stirring speech from *The Trojan War*, with tears in his eyes.

Polonius is ordered to take good care of the actors.

Let them be well used, for they are the abstract and brief chronicles of the time.[3]

My lord, I will use them according to their desert.[4]

Like most people, Polonius looks down on actors. Hamlet reminds him that they deserve respect.

Dost thou hear me, old friend? Can you play *The Murder of Gonzago*?

Ay, my lord.

You could for a need study a speech of some dozen or sixteen lines, which I would set down and insert in't, could you not?

Ay, my lord.

Hamlet speaks to the lead actor and sets his plan in motion. He has chosen tomorrow night's play very carefully...

1. uncurrent: without value.   2. cracked within the ring: broken (a play on words referring to the fact that a coin of the time would be made worthless if it was cracked from the edge to the ring surrounding the monarch's portrait, as well as encouraging the youth not to let his voice crack onstage—"within the ring").   3. abstract . . . time: short summary of the way things are.   4. use them according to their desert: treat them as they deserve.

Is it not monstrous that this player here, but in a fiction, in a dream of passion...

...could force his soul so to his own conceit that from its working all his visage wanned.[1]

How can an actor feign such real passion?

Left alone, Hamlet bursts out angrily.

What would he do, had he the motive and the cue for passion that I have? He would drown the stage with tears.

He compares his own situation.

Yet I, a dull and muddy-mettled[2] rascal, peak,[3] like John-a-dreams,[4] unpregnant of my cause,[5] and can say nothing.

Am I a coward? That I, the son of a dear father murdered... must unpack my heart with words[6]...

I have heard that guilty creatures sitting at a play have, by the very cunning of the scene...

...been struck so to the soul that presently they have proclaimed their malefactions.[7]

Why can't he take action?

I'll have these players play something like the murder of my father before mine uncle... If he do blench,[8] I know my course.

This is the answer!

The play's the thing wherein I'll catch the conscience of the king.

If Claudius' reaction to the play betrays guilt, Hamlet will know what to do.

1. all his visage wanned: his whole face grew pale.   2. muddy-mettled: dull-spirited.   3. peak: mope.
4. John-a-dreams: nickname for a dreamy person.   5. unpregnant of my cause: slow to act.   6. unpack my heart with words: do nothing but talk.   7. malefactions: wrongdoings.   8. blench: flinch and turn aside.

A Trap Is Set

"He does confess he feels himself distracted, but from what cause he will by no means speak."

Rosencrantz and Guildenstern admit that they do not know what is wrong with Hamlet.

"Nor do we find him forward to be sounded[1] but, with a crafty madness, keeps aloof."

"It so fell out that certain players we o'er-raught[2] on the way. And there did seem in him a kind of joy."

They tell the queen that the actor's passion pleased Hamlet.

"They have already been ordered this night to play before him."

Claudius is glad to hear about the play.

"Sweet Gertrude, leave us too, for we have closely[3] sent for Hamlet hither, that he, as 'twere by accident, may here affront[4] Ophelia."

But now it's time to put Polonius' plan into action.

"Her father and myself, lawful espials,[5] will so bestow[6] ourselves that, seeing unseen, we may of their encounter frankly judge."

"I hear him coming. Let's withdraw, my lord."

They'll see if Hamlet has gone mad out of love for Ophelia.

"Read on this book, that show of such an exercise may color your loneliness.[7]"

"We are oft to blame in this, that with devotion's visage[8] and pious action we do sugar o'er the devil himself.[9]"

Polonius is reminded that people often conceal badness by pretending to be good.

"O, 'tis too true! How smart a lash that speech doth give my conscience!"

These words mean something to Claudius!

1. forward to be sounded: eager to be questioned.   2. o'er-raught: overtook.   3. closely: privately, secretly.
4. affront: come face to face with.   5. espials: spies.   6. bestow: position.   7. show . . . loneliness: if you pretend
to read, Hamlet will not think it odd that you are by yourself.   8. devotion's visage: an appearance of devoutness.
9. sugar . . . himself: hide bad deeds with sweetness.

To be, or not to be?[1] That is the question.

Whether 'tis nobler in the mind to suffer the slings and arrows of outrageous fortune...

...or to take arms against a sea of troubles, and by opposing end them.

Hamlet's distress and confusion continues. Is it worth living?

For who would bear the whips and scorns of time...

...when he himself might his quietus make[3] with a bare bodkin?[4]

Is dying any worse than going to sleep?

Ay, there's the rub,[2] for in that sleep of death what dreams may come?

To die, to sleep. To sleep, perchance to dream.

But what may happen after death—nightmares?

The problems of life could be ended so quickly.

But that the dread of something after death...puzzles the will[5]...

...and makes us rather bear those ills we have than fly to others that we know not of.

The fear of what happens after death makes people live with their problems, rather than taking their own life.

Thus conscience does make cowards of us all.

The turmoil in his mind prevents him from taking his revenge.

1. to be or not to be: to live or to die. 2. there's the rub: that's the problem. 3. his quietus make: free himself.
4. a bare bodkin: a mere dagger. 5. puzzles the will: stops us in confusion.

NOT MAD FOR LOVE

Just then, he sees Ophelia. He thinks she is reading a prayerbook.

The fair Ophelia! Nymph, in thy orisons[1] be all my sins remembered.

She tries to return his letters and love tokens.

My lord, I have remembrances[2] of yours that I have longed to re-deliver.

She recalls happier times.

Take these again, for to the noble mind rich gifts wax poor[3] when givers prove unkind.

I did love you once.

Indeed, my lord, you made me believe so.

But then he turns on her.

Get thee to a nunnery. Why wouldst thou be a breeder of sinners?

We are arrant knaves[4] all, believe none of us.

O, help him, you sweet heavens!

Or if thou wilt needs marry, marry a fool...

...for wise men know well enough what monsters you make of them.

God hath given you one face and you make yourselves another.

I say we will have no more marriage. Those that are married already, all but one shall live[5]—the rest shall keep as they are.

Hamlet blames all women for men's unhappiness. They should become nuns and have no more children. He's really thinking about his mother.

Women use makeup to trick men.

His feelings all relate to his mother.

1. orisons: prayers.   2. remembrances: keepsakes, gifts.   3. wax poor: become worthless.
4. arrant knaves: despicable men.   5. all but one shall live: all married couples apart from one shall live on. Hamlet is referring to Claudius and Gertrude; he intends to end their marriage violently.

To a nunnery, go.

O, what a noble mind is here o'erthrown! O, woe is me, t'have seen what I have seen.

Love! His affections do not that way tend, nor what he spake, though it lacked form a little,[1] was not like madness.

Claudius now knows that Hamlet is not in love with Ophelia—but neither is he mad.

There's something in his soul, o'er which his melancholy sits on brood.[2]

Claudius knows that trouble lies ahead.

I have in quick determination thus set it down: he shall with speed to England.

He decides to get rid of Hamlet by sending him to England.

After the play, let his queen mother all alone entreat[3] him to show his grief...

...and I'll be placed, so please you, in the ear of all their conference.[4]

It shall be so. Madness in great ones must not unwatch'd go.

Polonius is still not convinced. He has another plan. Perhaps the queen can persuade Hamlet to reveal his problem?

Reluctantly, Claudius agrees.

1. lacked form a little: made little sense.   2. sits on brood: broods over, like a hen hatching eggs.
3. entreat: beg.   4. in the ear of all their conference: within earshot of their conversation.

THE PLAY

Speak the speech, I pray you... trippingly on the tongue.[1]

Hamlet wants the actors to behave naturally and not to overact or shout.

Be not too tame neither, but let your own discretion be your tutor.

I prithee,[2] when thou seest that act afoot, even with the very comment of thy soul, observe mine uncle.

Horatio must watch Claudius carefully during the murder scene.

"Both here and hence pursue me lasting strife, If, once a widow, ever I be wife!"

"So think thou wilt no second husband wed, but die thy thoughts when thy first lord is dead."

In the play, the queen declares she would never marry again, but the king says he knows better.

Have you heard the argument?[3] Is there no offence in't?[4]

No, no, they do but jest.

Claudius is getting uneasy.

What do you call the play?

The Mousetrap.

He poisons him in the garden.

You shall see anon[5] how the murderer gets the love of Gonzago's wife.

Give me some light. Away!

Claudius stops the play.

1. trippingly on the tongue: as you would speak naturally.   2. prithee: beg you.   3. argument: the plot of the play.
4. Is there no offence in't?: Are you sure there's nothing insulting in it?   5. anon: soon.

This convinces Hamlet that the ghost told the truth.

O good Horatio, didst perceive?[1]...

...upon the talk of the poisoning?

Very well, my lord.

Come, some music! Come, the recorders!

The king, sir, is in his retirement marvelous distempered.[2]

The king and queen are upset.

The queen...in most great affliction of spirit,[3] hath sent me to you.

She desires to speak with you in her closet[4] ere[5] you go to bed.

Good my lord, what is your cause of distemper?

Sir, I lack advancement.[6]

Asked to explain himself, Hamlet pretends he's angry at not inheriting the throne.

O, the recorders.

Will you play upon this pipe?

My lord, I cannot.

He teases Rosencrantz and Guildenstern.

'Tis as easy as lying—give it breath with your mouth and it will discourse most eloquent music.

Why, look you now, how unworthy a thing you make of me!

You would play upon me—do you think I am easier to be played on than a pipe?

Hamlet reveals that he knows what they have been up to.

I will speak daggers[7] to her, but use none.

Hamlet must speak plainly to his mother, but vows not to harm her, despite his anger.

1. didst perceive?: did you see?   2. distempered: angry.   3. affliction of spirit: dismay.
4. closet: private room.   5. ere: before.   6. I lack advancement: I am not moving up in the world (i.e., I am not king).
7. speak daggers: speak angrily.

MISTAKEN IDENTITY

I like him not, nor stands it safe with us to let his madness range.

He to England shall along with you.

My lord, he's going to his mother's closet. Behind the arras I'll convey myself, to hear the process.[1]

O, my offence is rank; it smells to heaven. It hath the primal eldest curse[2] upon't, a brother's murder.

Claudius tells Rosencrantz and Guildenstern that they must take Hamlet to England. He's a danger to the kingdom.

Polonius plans to spy on Hamlet and his mother.

Claudius reflects on his guilt. A brother's murder is a terrible sin!

But, O, what form of prayer can serve my turn?

"Forgive me my foul murder?"

O wretched state! O bosom black as death! O limed[3] soul that, struggling to be free, art more engaged!

And now I'll do't. And so he goes to heaven. And so am I revenged.

Seeing Claudius at prayer, Hamlet contemplates murder.

And am I then revenged, to take him in the purging of his soul, when he is fit and seasoned for his passage?[4]

No!

But he decides against killing Claudius in prayer.

...that his soul may be as damned and black as hell, whereto it goes.

My words fly up, my thoughts remain below.

Words without thoughts never to heaven go.

Claudius knows that his prayers are in vain.

1. process: what goes on.   2. primal eldest curse: refers to Cain's murder of his brother Abel in the Bible.
3. limed: stuck in a trap.   4. to take . . . passage: to kill him in prayer, when his soul is cleansed and fit to go to heaven.

Tell him... your grace hath screen'd and stood between much heat and him.[1] I'll silence me e'en here.

Hamlet, thou hast thy father[2] much offended.

Mother, you have my father[3] much offended.

Hamlet refuses to refer to his stepfather Claudius as "father."

Gertrude is afraid of Hamlet.

You go not till I set you up a glass[4] where you may see the inmost part of you.

Thou wilt not murder me?

What, ho! Help, help!

How now! A rat?

O, I am slain!

The queen is horrified.

O, what a rash and bloody deed is this!

A bloody deed! Almost as bad, good mother, as kill a king and marry with his brother.

Hamlet has killed Polonius.

Intruding fool, farewell! I took thee for thy better.

Look here, upon this picture, and on this. This was your husband. Look you now, what follows.

He points to portraits of his father and uncle. How could she love Claudius?

Do not forget:

This visitation is but to whet thy almost blunted purpose.[5]

Do you see nothing there?

The ghost reminds Hamlet of his promise. Now Gertrude fears Hamlet really is mad.

O Hamlet, thou hast cleft my heart in twain.[6]

O, throw away the worser part of it, and live the purer with the other half.

1. your grace . . . him: you have protected him from a lot of trouble.
2. thy father: she means Claudius.   3. my father: he means old Hamlet.   4. set you up a glass: get you a mirror.
5. to whet thy almost blunted purpose: to remind Hamlet to aim his revenge at Claudius.
6. cleft my heart in twain: cut my heart in two.

HAMLET MUST GO

O heavy deed! It had been so with us,[1] had we been there.

This vile deed we must with all our majesty and skill both countenance[2] and excuse.

Hamlet in madness hath Polonius slain, and from his mother's closet hath he dragged him.

Go seek him out.

When Claudius hears of Polonius' death, he realizes that Hamlet cannot be left on the loose much longer.

Claudius is concerned that he will be blamed for this tragedy.

This sudden sending him away must seem deliberate pause[3]...

Diseases desperate grown by desperate appliance are relieved, or not at all.

Where is Polonius?

In heaven—send thither to see.

If your messenger find him not there, seek him i'th'other place[4] yourself.

But indeed, if you find him not...you shall nose[5] him as you go up the stairs into the lobby.

Hamlet taunts Claudius by answering him flippantly, in riddles.

Claudius has to get rid of Hamlet, but it must look convincing.

Hamlet, this deed, for thine especial safety...must send thee hence with fiery quickness.

The bark[6] is ready and the wind at help. The associates tend, and everything is bent for England.

For England?

Our sovereign process,[7] which imports at full[8]...

...the present death of Hamlet.

Claudius claims he is sending Hamlet away for his own safety.

A ship is waiting to take him to England right away.

A secret letter instructs the king of England to have Hamlet murdered!

1. It had been so with us: He would have killed me.   2. countenance: accept.
3. pause: consideration.   4. th'other place: hell.   5. nose: smell.   6. bark: ship.
7. sovereign process: royal order.   8. imports at full: gives full instructions for.

28

The Norwegian army is marching across Denmark, as arranged earlier.

On the way to the harbor, Hamlet meets some soldiers.

The captain admits that their mission is fairly pointless.

Why can't he just get on with it?

He vows to act.

1. whose . . . purposed?: whose army is this? What is their mission?
2. This thing's to do: This thing has yet to be done.   3. sith: since.

OPHELIA'S TRAGEDY

I will not speak with her.

She is importunate, indeed distract.[1]

Back at court, Ophelia begs to see the queen.

"He is dead and gone, lady, He is dead and gone. At his head a grass-green turf, At his heels a stone."

The shock of her father's death has affected her mind.

"Tomorrow is Saint Valentine's day, All in the morning betime,[2] And I a maid at your window, To be your Valentine."

Pretty Ophelia!

Follow her close. Give her good watch,[3] I pray you.

Even Claudius is affected by Ophelia's distress.

O, this is the poison of deep grief. It springs all from her father's death.

When sorrows come, they come not single spies but in battalions.[4] First, her father slain...

Next, your son gone...poor Ophelia.

The situation worsens. One tragedy follows another.

Last, and as much containing as all these,[5] her brother is in secret come from France...

Laertes has returned...

...and wants not buzzers[6] to infect his ear with pestilent speeches[7] of his father's death.

...and it seems he blames Claudius for his father's death.

Save yourself, my lord. Young Laertes, in a riotous head, o'erbears your officers.

They cry, "Choose we:[8] Laertes shall be king!"

There's a commotion outside.

1. importunate, indeed distract: insisting, in fact out of her mind.   2. betime: early.
3. Give her good watch: Watch her carefully.   4. they come . . . battalions: (sorrows) come one after the other,
in large groups.   5. Last, and . . . these: Last, but not least.   6. wants not buzzers: is not short of rumor-mongers.
7. pestilent speeches: disrespectful talk.   8. Choose we: Let us choose.

O thou vile king, give me my father!

Before they can move, Laertes bursts in.

Tell me, Laertes, why thou art thus incensed.

Claudius calms him down.

Where is my father?

Dead.

But not by him.

Is't possible a young maid's wits should be as mortal as[1] an old man's life?

Before he can explain, Ophelia appears once again.

There's rosemary, that's for remembrance...

...and there is pansies, that's for thoughts.

I would give you some violets, but they withered all when my father died.

Laertes can't believe what he is seeing.

Do you see this, O God?

If by direct or by collateral hand they find us touched,[2] we will our kingdom give.

Claudius says others should judge whether he was involved in Polonius' death.

His means of death, his obscure funeral[3]...cry to be heard. I must call't in question.

Laertes agrees, but is angry that his father's funeral was such a paltry affair.

So you shall. And where the offence is, let the great axe fall.

Claudius agrees. Laertes seems satisfied for the moment...

1. as mortal as: as vulnerable as.   2. If by . . . touched: If they decide that I was directly or indirectly involved.
3. obscure funeral: secret funeral, without proper ceremony.

HAMLET'S ESCAPE

There's a letter for you, sir. It came from the ambassador that was bound for England.

Messengers bring Horatio a letter from Hamlet.

"Ere we were two days old at sea, a pirate of very warlike appointment[1] gave us chase..."

Hamlet tells how he escaped the ship to England.

and in the grapple I boarded them. On the instant they got clear of our ship, so I alone became their prisoner.

The pirates let Hamlet go because they had an errand for him.

He which hath your noble father slain pursued my life.[2]

But tell me why you proceeded not[3] against these feats.

Meanwhile, in the king's chamber, Claudius tells Laertes that Hamlet tried to kill him, too.

The queen his mother lives almost by his looks.

The other motive... is the great love the general gender[4] bear him.

He invents reasons for not bringing Hamlet to justice.

And so have I a noble father lost, a sister driven into desperate terms[5]...

...but my revenge will come.

Laertes believes him, and wants revenge—exactly as Claudius planned.

"Tomorrow shall I beg leave to see your kingly eyes, when I shall, first asking your pardon...

...thereunto recount the occasion of my sudden and more strange return."

Claudius receives Hamlet's letter.

1. of very warlike appointment: very aggressive, as if at war.　2. pursued my life: tried to kill me.　3. proceeded not: took no action.　4. general gender: common people.　5. desperate terms: an extreme or hopeless state.

But let him come. It warms the very sickness in my heart that I shall live and tell him to his teeth, "Thus diest thou."

Laertes welcomes the confrontation.

Laertes, was your father dear to you?

Why ask you this?

Hamlet comes back. What would you undertake to show yourself in deed your father's son more than in words?

To cut his throat in the church.

Claudius goads Laertes, trying to make him angrier still.

A fencing match is to be arranged, and Laertes will have a sharpened blade.

He, being remiss[1]... and free from all contriving, will not peruse the foils.[2]

Laertes will poison the point of his rapier.

I'll touch my point with this contagion.[3]

Claudius plans to have a poisoned cup at the ready, too.

A chalice[4]... whereon but sipping...

One woe doth tread upon another's heel,[5] so fast they follow. Your sister's drowned, Laertes.

Gertrude brings news of yet another tragedy: Ophelia is dead.

How much I had to do to calm his rage!

Now fear I this will give it start again.

Laertes is in despair. Claudius' plotting may not have been necessary.

1. remiss: trusting.   2. peruse the foils: check the swords.   3. contagion: poison.   4. chalice: cup.
5. One woe . . . heel: One tragedy follows right after another.

A Secret Funeral

Is she to be buried in Christian burial when she wilfully seeks her own salvation?[1]

This might be the pate[2] of a politician, which this ass now o'erreaches.[3]

Who is to be buried in't?

One that was a woman, sir, but rest her soul, she's dead.

The gravediggers aren't sure it's right to bury a suspected suicide in holy ground.

Hamlet contemplates the skulls.

How long hast thou been a grave-maker?

I came to't...the very day that young Hamlet was born, he that is mad and sent into England.

Why was he sent to England?

He shall recover his wits there or, if he do not, it's no great matter there—there the men are as mad as he.

This same skull, sir, was Yorick's skull, the king's jester.

Alas, poor Yorick. I knew him, Horatio.

He hath borne me on his back a thousand times, and now how abhorred in my imagination it is![4]

Where be your gibes[5] now, your gambols, your songs?

Now get you to my lady's chamber, and tell her, let her paint an inch thick, to this favor[6] she must come.

Make her laugh at that.

Not one now to mock your own grinning?

1. wilfully . . . salvation: takes her own life.   2. pate: head.
3. which . . . o'erreaches: the gravedigger is now the superior of the politician.
4. borne . . . it is: Hamlet used to ride on the jester's back, but now the jester's skeleton horrifies him.   5. gibes: jokes.   6. this favor: the skull's appearance.

Here comes the king, the queen, the courtiers. Who is this they follow?

I tell thee, churlish priest, a ministering angel shall my sister be, when thou liest howling.[3]

What ceremony else?[1]

We should profane the service of the dead...

...to sing sage requiem.[2]

What, the fair Ophelia!

Laertes is angry. There is to be no proper burial ceremony.

Sweets to the sweet... I hoped thou shouldst have been my Hamlet's wife.

Hold off the earth awhile, till I have caught her once more in mine arms.

This is I, Hamlet the Dane.

The devil take thy soul!

Laertes is overcome with grief.

Hamlet cannot restrain himself any longer.

I loved Ophelia. Forty thousand brothers could not with all their quantity of love make up my sum.

Good my lord, be quiet.

Pluck them asunder.[4]

Strengthen your patience in our last night's speech.[5]

1. What ceremony else?: Is this all there is to the funeral?   2. We should . . . reqiuem: We would be insulting the dead to mourn a suicide with a solemn burial service.   3. when thou liest howling: when you're screaming in hell.   4. Pluck them asunder: Pull them apart.   5. Strengthen . . . speech: Remember the plan we discussed last night, and be patient.

THE FENCING MATCH

You will lose, my lord... I will forestall their repair hither[1] and say you are not fit.

A courtier brings Laertes' challenge to Hamlet. To conceal his plot, the king has bet on Hamlet winning. Horatio is uneasy.

If it be now, 'tis not to come.[2] If it be not to come, it will be now... The readiness is all.

But Hamlet accepts the probability of death.

Give me your pardon, sir, I've done you wrong.

I am satisfied in nature...but in my terms of honor I stand aloof.

Hamlet makes peace but Laertes insists on honor being satisfied.

Hamlet scores the first hit.

A hit, a very palpable hit.

The king toasts Hamlet and then offers him the poisoned cup.

Here's to thy health.

I'll play this bout first; set it by awhile.

Our son shall win.

The queen carouses to thy fortune.[3]

Hamlet scores another hit. His mother is delighted. Claudius feigns pleasure.

Claudius is too late to stop the queen taking the poisoned cup.

Gertrude, do not drink!

I will, my lord. I pray you pardon me.

It is too late.

1. forestall . . . hither: ask them not to come.   2. to come: in the future.
3. carouses to thy fortune: drinks to your health.

Have at you now!

Part them. They are incensed.[1]

Nay, come again.

They accidentally swap swords.

They bleed on both sides. How is it, my lord?

How is't, Laertes?

O my dear Hamlet! The drink, the drink! I am poisoned.

Laertes, mortally wounded, confesses his treachery.

Let the door be locked. Treachery! Seek it out.

Why, as a woodcock to mine own springe,[2] I am justly killed with mine own treachery.

Hamlet wounds Laertes.

It is here, Hamlet... The treacherous instrument is in thy hand.

The point envenomed[3] too! Then, venom, to thy work.

Here, thou incestuous,[4] murderous, damned Dane, drink off this potion... Follow my mother.

Exchange forgiveness with me,[5] noble Hamlet...

At last, Hamlet knows what to do. He stabs the king...

...and forces him to drink the rest of the poison.

Laertes' last act is to make peace with Hamlet.

1. incensed: seething with rage.   2. as a woodcock to mine own springe: caught in my own trap, like a foolish bird.
3. envenomed: poisoned.   4. incestuous: referring to the fact that Claudius married his brother's wife.
5. Exchange forgiveness with me: Forgive me as I forgive you.

AN HONORABLE DEATH

Horatio, I am dead, thou livest. Report me and my cause aright to the unsatisfied.[1]

Hamlet begs Horatio to explain to everyone what really happened.

I am more an antique Roman than a Dane.[2] Here's yet some liquor left.

As th'art a man, Give me the cup! Let go, by heaven, I'll have't.

Horatio wants to die along with his friend, but Hamlet prevents him.

O God, Horatio, what a wounded name. Things standing thus unknown, shall live behind me[3]...

If thou didst ever hold me in thy heart, absent thee from felicity awhile,[4] and in this harsh world draw thy breath in pain, to tell my story.

Horatio must live to set the record straight, so that Hamlet is not dishonored.

Young Fortinbras, with conquest come from Poland, to the ambassadors of England gives this warlike volley.

There is gunfire outside.

Hamlet's last act is to approve the choice of Fortinbras as the new king of Denmark.

I do prophesy th'election lights on Fortinbras...

He has my dying voice[5]...

Now cracks a noble heart. Good night, sweet prince...

...and flights of angels sing thee to thy rest.

1. Report . . . unsatisfied: Reveal the truth to those who do not know.   2. more . . . Dane: ancient Romans preferred suicide to dishonor.   3. what a . . . behind me: my name would be dishonored if people in future times believed that I killed Claudius unjustly.   4. absent thee . . . awhile: put off the death you long for.   5. voice: vote. In death, Hamlet chooses Fortinbras to be the next king.

The Prince of Norway cannot believe his eyes—so many dead!

O proud death, what feast is toward in thine eternal cell,[1]...

...that thou so many princes at a shot so bloodily hast struck?

The English ambassador brings more sad news.

Rosencrantz and Guildenstern are dead.

Give order that these bodies high on a stage be placed to the view, and let me speak to th'yet unknowing world how these things came about.

Horatio volunteers to explain everything.

This is not how Fortinbras would have chosen to become king.

Let us haste to hear it... For me, with sorrow I embrace my fortune.

Bear Hamlet, like a soldier, to the stage. For he was likely, had he been put on,[2] to have proved most royal.

Hamlet's body is to be displayed ceremonially, like a hero's. He would have made a good soldier, and a good king.

Such a sight as this becomes the field, but here shows much amiss.[3] Go, bid the soldiers shoot.[4]

Death is expected on the battlefield, but in the royal palace it is a tragic sight.

1. what . . . cell: He imagines death feasting on the slain.   2. put on: put to the test.
3. shows much amiss: is out of place.   4. bid . . . shoot: fire the guns to salute
Hamlet's death.

The end 39

*W*illiam Shakespeare is probably the most famous playwright in the world, and yet little is known about his life. He left a will and some legal documents, but there was hardly anything written about him at the time to tell us what kind of man he was.

He was born in Stratford-upon-Avon, in the English Midlands, on April 23, 1564. His grandparents were farmers but his father, John, moved to town and became a glovemaker and wool trader. This made him quite a wealthy man, and by about 1570 he had become mayor of Stratford.

William was probably educated at the local grammar school, but did not go on to the university like other playwrights. Some people find this strange, because his plays are so full of complex language and clever plots. He also seems to have known several foreign languages, including Latin.

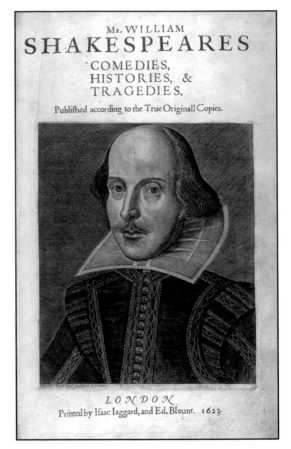

Portrait of Shakespeare by Martin Droeshout, on the title page of the First Folio edition of Shakespeare's plays (London, 1623).

MARRIAGE AND CHILDREN

In 1582 he married Anne Hathaway, the daughter of a local farmer, who was several years older than him and already pregnant. This was not unusual in those days, when marriages often took place only when the couple was sure there was a child on the way. Their daughter was christened Susanna, and then, in 1585, they had twins, Judith and Hamnet. Although that name seems significant in the light of Shakespeare's later play, Hamnet was named after a neighbor, Hamnet Sadler. Sadly, young Hamnet died of an illness at the age of eleven.

SHAKESPEARE'S CAREER

Soon after this, Shakespeare disappeared from Stratford and was not heard of again until 1592. No one knows where he went in those intervening years, and they are often called "the lost years."

One theory is that he became a schoolmaster to a wealthy family in Lancashire. Another is that he became a soldier and traveled abroad, which would explain his familiarity with countries like France and Italy, which appear in many of his plays.

Once he was established in the London theater, Shakespeare quickly became well-known—and quite wealthy. In 1597 he bought the second-biggest house in Stratford, New Place. All the time he was in London, Anne and the family stayed behind in Stratford. William probably visited them once a year or so, but it was only in 1614 that he went home for good.

His retirement did not last long, though: by 1616 he was dead. He is buried in Holy Trinity Church in Stratford, where the inscription on his gravestone reads:

"Blessed be the man that spares these stones,
And cursed be he that moves my bones."

OTHER PLAYS BY WILLIAM SHAKESPEARE

Note: We do not know the exact dates of most of Shakespeare's plays, or even the exact order in which they were written. The dates shown here are only approximate.

1590:   *Henry VI, Part I*
1591:   *Henry VI, Part II*
        Henry VI, Part III
1593:   *Richard III*
1594:   *Edward III**
        Titus Andronicus
        The Comedy of Errors
        The Taming of the Shrew
        The Two Gentlemen of Verona
1595:   *Love's Labor's Lost*
        Richard II
1596:   *King John*
        Romeo and Juliet
        A Midsummer Night's Dream
1597:   *The Merchant of Venice*
        The Merry Wives of Windsor
        Henry IV, Part I
1598:   *Henry IV, Part II*
1599:   *Much Ado About Nothing*
        As You Like It
        Julius Caesar
        Henry V
        Hamlet

1602:   *Twelfth Night*
1603:   *All's Well That Ends Well*
1604:   *Othello*
        Measure for Measure
1605:   *King Lear*
1606:   *Macbeth*
1608:   *Pericles*
        Coriolanus
        Timon of Athens
        Troilus and Cressida
        Antony and Cleopatra
1610:   *Cymbeline*
1611:   *The Winter's Tale*
        The Tempest
1613:   *Henry VIII***
1614:   *The Two Noble Kinsmen***

*May not actually be by Shakespeare
** By Shakespeare and John Fletcher

Shakespeare probably wrote two other plays, *Love's Labor's Won* and *Cardenio*, which have not survived.

SHAKESPEARE'S THEATER

When Shakespeare was a boy, plays were performed by groups of traveling actors or "players" who set up their stages in the town square or in the courtyard of an inn. By the time he started to write plays, however, the first permanent theaters were being built in London. The first was The Theater, built in 1576 on the north bank of the river Thames.

Theaters were round wooden buildings with an open space in the middle and galleries of seats under a wooden roof. Hundreds of people packed in to see the plays. Those who could afford it sat in seats under cover, but most people paid a penny to stand in the open space. They were called "groundlings" and they were famous for their rowdy behavior. Because there was no electricity for lighting, plays could only be performed during daylight.

A cutaway view of The Globe theater in Southwark, London, where many of Shakespeare's plays were first performed.

Performances usually lasted about three hours, and it was quite usual for people to eat and drink during the play.

THE GLOBE

The theater that Shakespeare's company performed in was The Globe, on Bankside. The Globe was built in 1599 from the timbers of the old Theater in Shoreditch. When the lease for the old building ran out, the actors dismantled the theater during the night and moved it across the river. It burned down in 1613 during a performance of *Henry VIII*, when a spark from a cannon on stage set fire to the thatched roof.

ELIZABETHAN PLAYS

Elizabethan audiences loved excitement and spectacle: they wanted to be entertained, and they liked variety. Theater managers had to keep them happy, as Shakespeare was very well aware. This meant that theaters needed a constant supply of new plays and new writers. Often, several writers worked together on one play, each writing the parts they were good at.

The main types of play were tragedies (about the downfall of heroic men) and comedies (which were lighthearted and ended happily ever after, but weren't necessarily funny). There were also pastoral plays (about shepherds and simple country life) and historical plays, which reminded people about the great heroes of the past, particularly English kings. Shakespeare could and did turn his hand to any of these, and some of his plays combine elements of several styles.

REVENGE PLAYS

When Shakespeare was writing *Hamlet*, plays about revenge were very fashionable. They usually involved a grisly murder, ghosts, poison, people in disguise—and a lot of dead bodies at the end. Some of the better ones were *The Revenger's Tragedy*, *The Spanish Tragedy*, and *The Malcontent*, but others were just an excuse for a bloodbath. *Hamlet* was certainly following the trend, but Shakespeare went one better by having Hamlet tell us what he was thinking and why he was doing (or not doing) things. This was quite new in Elizabethan theater.

THE PLAYERS IN *HAMLET*

Shakespeare's writing about the traveling players in *Hamlet* tells us a lot about the theater of his time. First, they can perform any kind of play, as Polonius tells us: "tragedy, comedy, history, pastoral, pastoral-comical, historical-pastoral, tragical-historical…" Because women were not allowed to perform in public, the female roles in Elizabethan plays were played by boys whose voices had not yet broken. Hamlet teases the boy player about growing up because it means that he might soon be out of a job. Hamlet regards the actors with affection, but Polonius looks down on them. Most Elizabethans regarded traveling actors as not much more than tramps, and possibly criminals. The authorities didn't like them because plays attracted large gatherings of people, including thieves and pickpockets.

Hamlet's advice to the players tells us that some of the "stars" of his day were inclined to overact: they waved their arms about and spoke very loudly. Some of the comic actors also used to throw in their own jokes or comic routines to get a laugh. Shakespeare is against this – he wants a more natural kind of acting. After all, he says in *Hamlet*, acting is "holding a mirror up to nature"—showing us ourselves and the times we live in. It's amazing that his plays still do this after 400 years.

SOME *HAMLET* FACTS

• Denmark was always competing with Sweden for control of the Baltic. Perhaps this inspired all the talk about preparing for war in *Hamlet*.

• There have been several female Hamlets, including Sarah Siddons (1775), Sarah Bernhardt (1899), Frances de la Tour (1980), and Angela Winkler (2000).

• Thomas Betterton first played Hamlet in 1660 and went on playing him for fifty years, until he was 74. The youngest Hamlet was Master Betty, who played the role in 1805 at the age of 13.

• Shakespeare himself is supposed to have played the Ghost in his own production.

HAMLET

Shakespeare probably wrote both *Hamlet* and *Julius Caesar* around 1598 or 1599. *Hamlet* was registered for printing in 1602, and we know that a play called *Hamlet* was on stage in 1600.

Many of the playwrights of Shakespeare's day "borrowed" stories from earlier plays or poems. Some of these were already very old and some had been translated from French, Italian, or Spanish.

AN ANCIENT LEGEND

The story of Hamlet was first written down by Saxo Grammaticus at the end of the 12th century. It was published in English in 1514. But it was already an old tale by the time Saxo wrote it down: stories of a "mad" prince avenging his father appear in ancient Scandinavian legends.

THE ORIGINAL HAMLET STORY

Two brothers, Horwendil and Feng, rule the province of Jutland for the King of Denmark. Feng kills his brother and then marries his widow, Gerutha. Her son Amleth is too young to take proper revenge on his uncle, so he pretends to be insane and goes around covered in dirt and speaking nonsense. He kills a friend of Feng's who is eavesdropping in the queen's bedroom, cuts up his body and feeds it to pigs. Amleth is sent to England but returns one year later, just as the court is celebrating his funeral. He burns down the banqueting hall. While Amleth pretended to be insane, his sword was nailed to its scabbard to prevent him harming himself. Now he swaps his sword with his uncle's. He wakes Feng, who grabs the nearest sword but cannot draw it. Amleth kills his uncle with Feng's own weapon. Amleth explains his actions and is elected king. He is eventually killed in battle by the new Danish king. He dies a hero's death.

WHAT WAS SHAKESPEARE'S SOURCE?

In Shakespeare's time, a French writer called Belleforest included the Hamlet story in his collection of "Tragic Histories." He made the story more sensational and added the Ophelia character and the ghost. These tales were hugely popular throughout Europe, and Shakespeare must have known about them. But could he read them in French?

Records also show that there was a stage version of *Hamlet* before Shakespeare's, possibly by a dramatist called Thomas Kyd. He was famous for another play about revenge called *The Spanish Tragedy.* This Hamlet play was never printed and has disappeared, but if it was on stage in the 1590s, Shakespeare almost certainly would have seen it.

So, Belleforest based his story on a translation of Saxo; an anonymous playwright read Belleforest's story and wrote his own play; Shakespeare saw that play—and thought he could write a better one…

1558
Elizabeth, daughter of Henry VIII, becomes Queen of England.

1564
William Shakespeare is born on April 23 in Stratford-upon-Avon, Warwickshire.

1572
Parliament passes a law regarding the punishment of vagrants (tramps). This includes actors.

1576
The Theater, the first permanent playhouse in London, is built in Shoreditch, on the north side of the river Thames.

1582
Shakespeare marries Anne Hathaway.

1583
Shakespeare's daughter Susanna is born.

1585
Birth of Shakespeare's twins, Hamnet and Judith.
A troupe of English actors performs in Denmark.

1587
Mary, Queen of Scots, is executed after being implicated in a plot to murder Queen Elizabeth.

1588
The Spanish Armada is defeated and England saved from invasion.

1592
An outbreak of plague closes the playhouses; instead of plays, Shakespeare writes poems and sonnets.

1594
The playhouses reopen. Shakespeare joins The Lord Chamberlain's Men as actor and playwright.

1596
Shakespeare's son Hamnet dies, aged 11.

1597
Shakespeare buys New Place, the second-biggest house in Stratford.

1599
The Globe opens on Bankside. Shakespeare is a "sharer" or stockholder. He writes *Hamlet*.

1603
Queen Elizabeth dies without an heir. James VI of Scotland becomes king of England, taking the title James I. His wife, Anne of Denmark, is queen.

1605
The Gunpowder Plot, a conspiracy to assassinate James I and his Parliament, is foiled on November 5.

1606
King Christian IV of Denmark pays a state visit to London. He sees three plays, possibly including *Hamlet*.

1613
Shakespeare's Globe theater is destroyed by fire but rebuilt the following year.

1616
William Shakespeare dies in Stratford on April 23.

1623
Two of Shakespeare's former theatrical colleagues publish the *First Folio*, a collected edition of his dramatic works.

By the mid-16th century, the kingdoms of Norway and Denmark had been more or less united for some years. Sweden had broken away in 1521. Elsinore (Helsingør), where Shakespeare sets *Hamlet*, is a city in eastern Denmark.

In Shakespeare's time, Denmark was ruled by Frederick II (ruled 1559–1588) and then his son Christian IV (ruled 1588–1648).

Until 1660, Denmark was an elective monarchy. This means that a prince did not become king just by birthright, but had to be voted in by the nobles at court. In most cases the nobles voted for the prince anyway, but in *Hamlet* this has not happened. Claudius has been elected instead, although we never discover why. This is odd, because Claudius tells us that Hamlet is popular with the people and even Fortinbras praises him.

WHAT DID THE ELIZABETHANS KNOW ABOUT DENMARK?

We can't be sure what Shakespeare knew about Denmark. He sets *Twelfth Night* in "Bohemia," for example, but gives it a coastline, which Bohemia does not really have. Sometimes he uses distant countries to convey somewhere romantic and exciting. In the old legends, Denmark is a grim, barbaric place. None of the later versions of the Hamlet story gives any description of what the country is like. Shakespeare's depiction of Denmark shows us a modern, sophisticated court with educated people.

The Elizabethans knew quite a lot about modern Denmark because the King of Scotland, James VI, had married Anne of Denmark, sister of Christian IV, in 1589. The fact that James had braved hazardous sea journeys to bring her home to Scotland had been much talked about. Since James was the likely successor to Queen Elizabeth (he became James I of England in 1603), the English were naturally curious about Anne's homeland.

There were good relations between the two countries. A royal delegation went to Elsinore in 1605 to give Christian IV the Order of the Garter, England's highest honor. Christian visited London himself in 1606, during which time three plays were performed for him—perhaps including *Hamlet*.

There were cultural connections, too: Christian loved music and plays. The English lute-player John Dowland spent many years at the Danish court, as court musician and composer, between 1598 and 1606. Dowland would have brought back news of Denmark.

WAS SHAKESPEARE AT ELSINORE?

We know that troupes of English actors traveled abroad, and that in 1585–1586 such a group visited Denmark. Three of the actors are mentioned by name, and one of these at least, William Kemp, was in the same company as Shakespeare. No one knows where Shakespeare was between 1585 and 1592, so it's possible that he may have visited Elsinore. This could have been the inspiration for *Hamlet*.

HAMLET ON STAGE AND SCREEN

amlet is the role that all great actors most want to play. The actor who played Hamlet in Shakespeare's production was Richard Burbage. He was the company's leading actor and took most of the tragic roles. He was probably about 33 at the time. In the 18th century, David Garrick gave rather sensational performances but cut down a lot of the speeches. Two great Hamlets of the 19th century were John Philip Kemble, who played him as a sad, serious figure, and Edmund Kean, who was passionate and exciting. Other great Hamlets have included Laurence Olivier and John Gielgud (1930s) and Paul Scofield (1950s). In the 1960s David Warner played him as a real student of the 1960s, with a long woolly scarf and glasses. *Doctor Who* star David Tennant played Hamlet to great critical acclaim in 2008.

HAMLET ON SCREEN

There have been several film versions of *Hamlet*, and many more films and plays loosely based on the story. Traditional versions include those starring Laurence Olivier (1948), Richard Burton (1964), Mel Gibson (1990), and Kenneth Branagh (1996). A more unusual version is *Hamlet 2000*, set in modern-day New York and starring Ethan Hawke. American director Joe Papp's 1990 version starring Kevin Kline was first produced on stage, then recorded for TV.

One of the most original spin-offs is a play by Tom Stoppard, *Rosencrantz and Guildenstern Are Dead*. These two minor characters take the lead, commenting on the action of the play as if they're not sure why they're in it.

HAMLET AND ELSINORE

Today, *Hamlet* brings thousands of tourists to Elsinore. You can walk down Ophelia Way, sleep at the Hamlet Hotel, and see a production of the play in the courtyard of Kronborg Castle, where it is staged every year.

Laurence Olivier directed and starred in the famous 1948 version of Hamlet, *a Two Cities Films production.*

INDEX

A
actors 42, 43, 47

B
Belleforest 44
Burbage, Richard 47

C
Christian IV 46
Claudius 46

D
Denmark 43, 44, 46

E
Elizabethans 42, 46
Elsinore 46, 47

F
films 47

G
Ghost 43
Globe theater 42
groundlings 42

H
Hamlet (prince) 43, 44, 46
Hamlet (play) 43, 44, 46, 47
Hathaway, Anne 40
Helsingør *see* Elsinore
Henry VIII 42
Holy Trinity church, Stratford 41

J
James VI of Scotland (James I of England) 46
Julius Caesar 44

K
Kemp, William 46

M
movies 47

N
Norway 46

O
Ophelia 44

P
Polonius 43

R
revenge plays 43

S
Saxo Grammaticus 44
Shakespeare, William 40, 41, 42, 43, 44
Spanish Tragedy, The 44
Stratford-upon-Avon 40–41
Sweden 43, 46

T
television 47
tragedies 42
Twelfth Night 46